FIRST DAY CRITTER JITTERS

gulp.

written by
Jory John

illustrated by
Liz Climo

Dial Books
for Young Readers

Trust me, you *don't* want to be late on the first day of school.

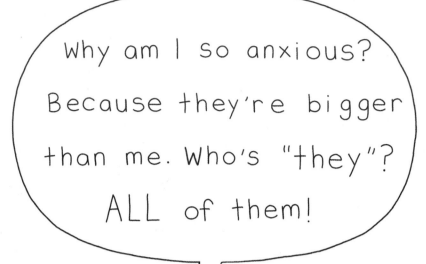

gulp.

Maybe next year I'll be ready.

I'm feeling skittish. Here's why: I have a tendency to repeat things that other animals say. Like, one time, somebody said to me, "Please stop talking, just this once," and then I kept repeating, "Please stop talking, just this once, please stop talking, just this once, please stop talking, just this once, please stop talking..."

I have a feeling that's not going to fly at school.

So, yeah... I've already been traveling toward the bus stop for twenty minutes and I'm still at my front door. I should really learn how to ride a bike. Sheesh.

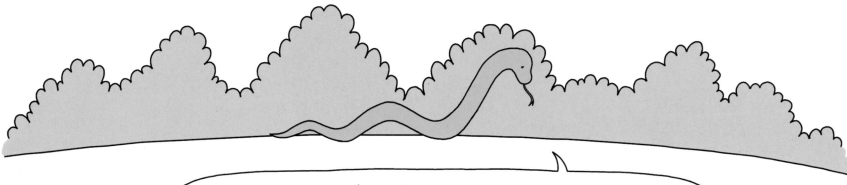

Bye-bye, backpack. Sniff. Bye-bye, lunch. Sniff. Bye-bye, art supplies. Sniff.

I'm exhausted. Aren't I supposed to be hibernating right now?

...can't stop hopping, so much energy, can't stop hopping, so much energy, can't stop hopping, so much...

My eyelids... won't... stop... closing...

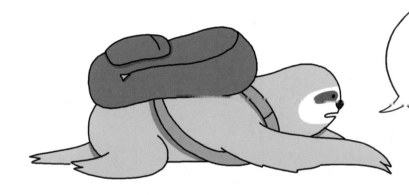

...I'm almost to the sidewalk... I can do this... just a few more blocks to go...yes...feel the burn...

Right now, my mom and I would be reading a book together and drinking hot chocolate with marshmallows. Do buses have hot chocolate?

Excuse me? Do you know what that rock is doing up there?

Ah, well, yes. I feel a bit silly about this, but I have *plenty* to be nervous about. The truth is, I'm rather forgetful. What if I can't remember all of your names? What if I forget the last thing I said? What if I can't recall where I put the chalk?

Don't worry, Mr. Sherwood! I may be a tiny mouse, but I have the memory of an *elephant!* And I'll help you remember our names using a mnemonic device! For example, my name is *Chauncy* and I like *cheese.* See how that works?

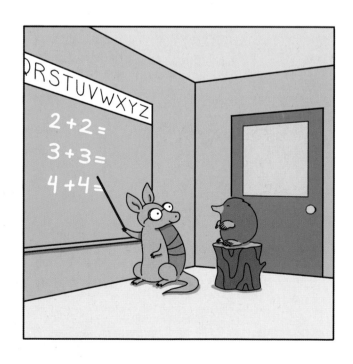

The next day . . .

To Alyssa, of course —J.J.

For Kathleen —L.C.

Dial Books for Young Readers
An imprint of Penguin Random House LLC, New York

Text copyright © 2020 by Jory John
Illustrations copyright © 2020 by Liz Climo.

Visit us online at penguinrandomhouse.com

Library of Congress Cataloging-in-Publication Data is available.

Printed in China • ISBN 9780735228559

Special Markets ISBN 9780593354704 Not for Resale

3 5 7 9 10 8 6 4 2

Design by Lily Malcom • Text handlettered and set in Rockwell

The illustrations in the book were done with digital magic.

This Imagination Library edition is published by Penguin Young Readers, a division
of Penguin Random House, exclusively for Dolly Parton's Imagination Library,
a not-for-profit program designed to inspire a love of reading and learning, sponsored
in part by The Dollywood Foundation. Penguin's trade editions of this work are
available wherever books are sold.